PROLOGUE

The pandemic has left the streets of New Orleans crawling with
the infected. Robberies, murders, and the constant risk of trans-
mission are a byproduct of the disease–the new norm. But it is beneath these layers of insanity, deep down in the primordial grime
beneath society where we find our humanity again.
These are the tales of the survivors. This is INFECTIOUS....

CASH FOR OLD

Part 2 of the INFECTIOUS Series

Created by

Briggs + Reeves

1

Looking in the window, we could see the robbery going down. We watched and listened, waiting to make a move.

The kid's voice snuck through the glass door of Crescent City Pawn. "Pull the guns out of the case and put them on the glass." The rat-faced kid honed in on Mickey. His finger wrapped around the trigger. "And do it slow."

Alexandre pressed closer to the window, blocking the glare. "Is that one of Victor's guys?"

The red and blue glow of the neon sign blocked my view of the gunman's face. Just below Alexandre's shoulder, I looked into the shop. "Victor would never hire a dirtbag like that."

Alexander wiped the white dust from under my nose. He rubbed it in his gums and focused on what was coming out of the pawnshop case. "Okay, Mickey, let's see how generous you're feeling tonight."

Stepping through the door, the kid with the piece glanced back.

"Looks like you're in a tight spot tonight there, huh Mick?"

"Yeah," Mickey said with the gun pressed into his head. "I'll be right with you after I help this customer. He's very interested in taking home your old revolver."

Alexander eyed a tool we had to put on ice with Mickey. "Well, he should be, it's a hell of a gun."

"I'll take that one too." The laughed and kid smiled back at us, before returning his attention to Mickey's forehead.

A single sweat droplet slipped from his dark brown hair onto his forehead. The round killing him exited through the droplet. It exploded in the glass pane next to the Mickey's face.

"But she's mine." Alexander smirked from behind the smoking gun. "And she only goes home with me."

The sun had disappeared from the sky. The hell on the streets of the last hour of fading daylight was over. They were all gone now, and it was safe again to walk the streets.

Alexandre's eyes pranced over the blued steel in his hand. Fresh out of lockup the wood grip fit snug to his sturdy hand. "Old Mickey, he didn't think we were any good for that loan. I could tell by that look in his eye he was shocked we were back in there so soon."

Walking past the Chateau, I felt like it was only yesterday my Alexandre rescued me from the clutches of that lunatic, Madam Honeydew. That psycho cunt was always playing with fire. She just made sure she was never the one who got burned. She was gonna get everybody killed, and I damn sure wasn't going to be a part of her little shop of whores.

"Tell you what, he didn't know whether to shit or go blind when I put that round through that kid's head."

Looking over the old brothel, I saw the light on in the third bedroom to the right. Somebody was getting paid. The problem was, it wasn't us. But you know what, that's fine. Even with the streets dry right now because of this damn plague I wasn't gonna be kicking any of my hard-earned money back to that demon.

We had just spent most of our roll getting the tools out of hock. So, of course, we were tapped. God, I hated being broke. We had to get out of this life somehow.

"Why are you looking so sad, angel?"

"It's nothing," I told my Alexandre. "Just that feeling again."

"Well, you just lose that feeling as quick as you found it. We got ourselves a real winner here." He pulled the medical cards he picked out of the dead Mexican kid's pocket. "I can feel it in my bones." Alexandre put the gun in his pocket and began reading over the medical cards. "I gotta say, Mickey was awfully kind letting these walk."

I looked over the big mansions of the old-money neighborhood. We traipsed by like ghosts in the rising mist. "I would say he owed us after you saved his cheap ass. We don't get there when we do; he's got real problems."

"You're right about that. That kid had him dead to rights. A little pressure was all that separated that kid from being rich and being a stain on that shitty carpet." Alexander stared down the orange sight of the revolver. His long, muscular arm lined up the gun with a garden statue.

It was the house. The powder blue one with the ivy creeping up the turret was so gorgeous. Every time I went into Honeydews to drop off cash I'd sit and stare at it. I wanted that house. I just never knew how to make it mine.

"He should've wiped the note clean on the gun. He doesn't sell any of those damn things, anyway. He charges way too much." I always thought Mickey was a dickhead. Even after saving his life, he tried to run us up on the ten karat bands. That was just the tip of the iceberg for that scumbag.

"Ha, Mickey?" Alexander said, dropping the gun into his jacket pocket. "You're dreaming."

We continued walking. The beauty of the big houses had become ugly. It was like lava in my throat. Here we were flat broke, walking past these fenced mansions. We're out looking for people to rob, and these people have all this. It wasn't fair. We worked hard. We ground it out—up early in the mornings and out at late at night, dodging those zombies, and gambling on marks.

Why didn't we have a place like this monster with the stone wall out front? The smell of the blooming zinnias, decorating the gardens in orange fire and flame, was starting to make me sick.

"You all right, baby?"

I took a deep breath, shaking the nausea. It always seemed to follow me through this part of town. "I'm good."

Alexandre whipped out the old lady's medical card, waving it at me like it was some magic wand. "We take this lottery ticket and cash it in, and shortbread, we are good to go."

I nodded with my eyes closed, shaking the sickness. The street lights overhead dimmed. We continued away from the high walls of wonderland toward the boarded doors of the wasteland.

Alexandre looked back from the darkened streets in front of us. "I tell ya, I can't believe we made it through that neighborhood without getting fucked with. The cops always keep that place locked down."

I looked up at the beautiful brown eyes of my saving grace. There was only a tiny sparkle in the faint lights in the manicured streets behind us. "Maybe they were busy. I did hear somebody got shot at Mickey's."

The jobs were wearing on me. This skin was beautiful once. Now it was raw. That last asshole who thought he could put his hands on me left scratches all over my back and chest. Alexandre made sure he wouldn't do that again. After I got that watch off him, he whooped his ass good.

The stickups were getting to be too much. I didn't know if I was gonna get bit or poked by some SIL freak. I didn't know if the guy we were hitting was just some bum looking to score some quick skin. I just didn't know anything. Our methods were clean and precise after a year or so of practice. But the thought of not knowing where that next meal came from weighed on me. When the streets were dusty, and nobody wanted to come out, I could usually get something out of the tricks I kept in touch with from my days with Honeydew. Those could still be a little risky, but they paid. I always had Alexandre watching out close by. Because if Honeydew ever found out I was using her little black book, that bitch would slit my throat.

I was so tired of that line of work. I didn't want anyone touching me, but Alexandre. He may not be the smartest, but my God, look at that face. It was a miracle the day he walked into the Chateau. And it was even more a miracle both of us got lined up to work first shit.

The pre-work crowd and the bored housewives were the best. Yeah, they had time on their hands, which could make things weird after the work was done. But it seemed like the day-light always brought them back to their senses.

Her business model was great–for the buyers. It was like

delivering pizza. We'd be the ones who'd have to face the street. There was no risk of getting mugged or caught by the cops (like they cared). Customers had what they ordered, hot and ready on their front doorstep right when they wanted it.

Honeydew sent us out as meat. We'd do all the work, take all the risk. And then, she'd have the nerve to take a cut out of our ass.

That big house on St Phil's, that was my last one. It was right then and there with that psycho cunt with the slicked-back hair I knew I was destined for something much better. That's also when I pulled my beautiful Alexandre aside on those front steps and told him we'd have to get out on our own.

"I think this is the place, hon."

And that's just what we did.

Brackish brown water filled the dips in the street. Stuffed animals and pink plastic toys were tossed around the yard. Down the block, waves were still lapping against the foundations of the boarded corner houses. Rusted cars melted away into the cracked asphalt. "Wonder if this old lady is still alive in there?"

"I don't know, but it looks like the flood just let go of this place."

Alexandre read the license we snagged off the dead kid from the pawnshop. "Kid's name was Richard Suarez. Look at that terrible 'stache. What a dirtball?"

I looked down at the license. The kid looked better dead than he did alive. At least he didn't have that mean mug on his face anymore. "I just hope he was telling Mickey the truth about this place."

"Well, there's only one way to find out."

2

Trash from the receding waters littered the fenced lawn. The smell of still flood water and old garbage rose from the tight alley between the battered houses. Bloated trash bags oozed from their cans.

I could feel my cheeks puffed with the nausea. That same smell hit me every time we hit Bourbon Street. And I never got used to it.

"What's wrong?" Alexandre stood on top of a garbage can, peeking into the side window.

My hand covered my nose, blocking the rot. "That smell." I reached for what was left of the chain-link fence separating the two houses and tried not to gag. "It gets me every time."

Alexandre found a crack in a curtain alongside the house. He tried to peek inside to see our treasure. "I can't see much, but it looks dead in there." He stepped into the alley. "The kid could've stolen the cards from a hospital or something, but from what I can see, looks like the front door's booby-trapped. It sounded like a TV was on in there, too. But I didn't see anybody moving around."

"Maybe she's in the basement."

If this kid put the old lady from this card in the basement, she'd be lucky to be alive. Especially with the storms coming down on this neighborhood as of late. She'd probably smell like these garbage cans and look like what was coming out of the bags. This was starting to feel like another dead end.

Alexandre stepped away from the window and looked into the backyard. "I'm thinking we should at least check out the back."

I followed along, fighting the smell of the alley with my shirt. We came upon a pile of rusted medical equipment clogging the path to the back door. An undertow of the floodwaters had pulled wheelchairs and walkers against the corroded chain link.

I looked over the mangled heap of metal and plastic. "Maybe that kid wasn't lying."

"That's a shitload of equipment for just one old lady." Alexandre's eyes lit up as he dodged the decayed wheelchairs rushing toward the back door of the old shotgun house.

The surrounding houses in the forgotten section of town had been loosened from their foundations. The siding was rotted. The windows were broken. Porches were caved in. Paint rippled and cracked from the moisture of the receding waters and the hot days of summer. Bright orange spray-painted X's decorated doors and makeshift entryways next to pinned branches.

The waters stripped the glow of the metallic greens and fluorescent purples of the once lively neighborhood. The real estate gold around here had lost its shine. And the plants and trees were looking to take back what was theirs.

"This one's unlocked." Alexandre grabbed both the pistol and our old revolver from his pocket. He leaned against the loose siding and looked back at me. "You ready?"

I prepared myself for the worst. But after killing the in-house security, I was sure we'd be walking in on some little old lady in a wheelchair, not sure of who we were or what we were doing there. Mickey said the only preexisting condition was a touch of dementia, but she still used the bathroom herself. Those are self-sustaining statistics, right there. So when Mickey offered us the deal, it seemed like an easy choice.

Yeah, he had a little cash, but cash was cash. We'd spend it, and it was gone forever. He had some gold rings, which could mature over time if the world was gonna fall apart again. Or he had the old.

With the old, we could trade the pills. We could get kickbacks from treatments. We could get free meals delivered to the house for Christ's sake. It was a gold mine with endless opportunities.

We'd gotten hits in the past on old folks. But they never seemed to last very long. They would get too hard to take care of or they'd up and die on us. They were a useful commodity, but it took space and overhead to pull off the long-term stay. That just wasn't us. We were always on the move. We never had time to keep an eye on them. They'd get a sore on their ass, or find a way to fall and break something, and within a few days, our investment would be history.

For us, what the old brought in just never seemed to stretch very far–not without some out-of-pocket supplementation. What we needed was an old farm and time for some compounding interest. We just couldn't ever put enough of the pieces together to get the ball rolling.

From what we had heard, a dementia patient was a doctor's wet dream. They could milk insurance companies for constant testing, meds, transportation costs, treatment, special dietary additions, experimental pills, you name it. We just had to keep the old bat alive.

A whiff of mothballs hit hard as the door creaked open. Alexandre searched for more booby traps with the guns raised. Taking a step inside a tinge of rot, and canned ravioli slid in behind that initial chemical smell. A wave of his hand brought me further inside the door.

One last look around the bumpy backyard, and we were in.

3

"You smell that?"

A pungent whiff of the thick, stagnant air hit hard.

"Is that gas?"

There was a crack of a match followed by a whoosh of flame in the kitchen. The sound brought the stench of burnt hair.

The smell of iodine and aged cheddar crept up the open back basement steps. I wanted to gag but was too scared.

I clung to Alexandre's back as he leaned around the corner. A moan of pain climbed up the darkened steps pushing Alexandre toward the kitchen. There was no mildew. There was no rot. There was no smell leftover from the rising waters. The house was dry and warm. The wood floors in the camelback kitchen were all spotless. And there, at the stove, an old woman focused on a tall cast-iron pot.

The woman with the wrinkled rectangular jaw and the curly gray hair called out to us. "Ginny, Steve, y'all are late. Now y'all have a seat right there, and I don't wanna hear a word about the okra tonight."

"Hey Mona," a voice called from the front room. "You talking to yourself again?"

"There's more," I mouthed. Electricity filled the air of the dustless house. There were telltale signs of a possible strike. But whose ever it was, I'm sure was going to give it up easily.

Alexandre raised the handguns as the old woman continued her prep at the sink. We moved toward the doorway connecting the kitchen.

The folded plastic tips of the .410 shotgun shells and the copper-jacketed .380 slugs were all directed toward the front door where the faded Latin accent called out.

A white sheet dangled from the foot of a hospital bed, jutting into the doorway. The moan of pain grumbled again from the basement as I kept close to the small of Alexandre's back.

A collection of old folks looked up at the two of us. They eyed the guns and shook their heads in silence. All of my dreams flashed in front of my eyes. It was all happening. And it was just for us.

An old woman laid up in the center row of beds popped her head up. "You know you could hurt somebody with those things?"

I pressed my finger to my lips, hushing the old woman.

The old woman waved me off. "Yeah, yeah."

The voice from the front room called out again, drawing the handguns forward. "Mona, what are you doing back there?"

"I'm making dinner, you fool," the woman in the kitchen scolded. "Ginny and Steve just got home; soup's gonna be on soon. If you don't come back here and grab yourself some, it's gonna be all gone."

"Well then," the man's voice called out, "I best get myself back there and get some."

They all knew each other. They looked out for another. And they even cooked for one another. This was getting better with each room. I knew it was all going to come down to who it was we would have to kill. And I had a feeling he was sitting in the front room.

The grayed eyes turned from the firearm. Their bloated knuckles returned to crinkled newspapers and soft knitting. The man in the corner with the drool running down his chin winked at me. We moved toward the front of the house with the metallic powers of persuasion leading the way.

A creak in the weathered boards in the front sitting room sent a round from the revolver through the open doorway. The explosion, which sent my fingers into my ears, echoed off the compact plaster walls. The old farts sitting around the makeshift bedroom barely flinched.

Birdshot from the revolver had blown a plate-sized hole in

the front door. The old folks in the room rolled their eyes.

"Mona? Put that damn shotgun down," the voice called out. "I said I was coming, Godammit."

The gargled age in the man's voice raised Alexandre's handguns.

"Now, who in the hell's gonna fix that door?" the man grumbled, turning the corner.

He put eyes on Alexandre and pushed the walker with the green tennis balls past him. The moan from the basement called out through the floorboards again.

"Would somebody please bring Lenny his pills, and put his ass in that shower?" the man said, continuing his waddle toward the kitchen. "I can smell that summabitch from up here."

Alexandre and I watched as the old man marched by us. The piss and vinegar running through his veins dismissed the melonsized hole he narrowly avoided in his chest.

"How about you there, young man?" The old-timer passing by adjusting his glasses and stared at Alexandre. "Can you and your pretty girlfriend here go down and help him out. Those stairs are hell on these old knees."

Alexandre and I marched into the front room. A man in a wheelchair sat hand in hand with a woman wrapped in a knitted blanket. The white sheet covering her chest lifted as I checked to make sure they were breathing.

"That's Sally," Alexandre said.

"Who's Sally?"

"The woman from the medical cards. Look, that's her."

Sally Donaldson looked to be mostly comatose. The kid Alexandre put down in the pawnshop was full of shit. Because there was no way this lady was getting up to use the bathroom. It looked like the guy sitting next to her with the gold wedding band on must've done most of the heavy lifting for her.

"That's ten counting the guy in the basement," I told Alexandre as he checked the bear trap next to the front door. He looked back at me as the jagged iron jaws snapped shut. "Ten! Can you believe it? We're rich!"

I could hardly contain myself as I grabbed that beautiful face and slammed it into mine. My chest throbbed as I looked at the dollar signs laid up in the beds. The money from the sale of the pills alone from these geezers could put us anywhere we wanted in town. With the right doctor and the right insurance, not to mention whatever the government was dishing out to them on social security, we could live like royalty.

That knot in my chest, I had passed through that row of mansions disappeared. That feeling was something I'd carried with me since I was a little girl, and it was finally gone. This was our chance. We'd hit the big one.

"You go down and take care of that guy in the basement," I told Alexandre as I moved toward the bedsides. "I'm gonna check these people out. We gotta protect our investment here."

4

"So, how'd y'all get here?" I asked the old woman. Her puffy knuckles, wrapped in green veins, gripped the handle of the stainless ladle. Mixed vegetables and seafood in a reddish-brown sauce poured into flowered bowls pre-filled with rice.

The woman focused on the small hills of rice. "Come on, Ginny. I ain't got time for this. We need to get these folk's bellies filled."

"S'cuse me." The old man edged past me, forcing the walker into the kitchen. "If the two of you are just gonna stand around and chat, Sally and Phil are gonna die of starvation out there."

"Uh, honey?" Alexandre called from the basement. "You better get down here."

"Dammit." The green tennis balls came to a halt. "Did Lenny fall again? You tell his ass I said he can stay on that floor this time. Damn near threw my back, trying to pick him up."

The smell of the iodine thickened as I moved down the concrete steps. The moan called out into the darkness. I could see the glow of a single pull light dripping onto the basement floor. There, on the concrete slab, a man in a white gown laid on his side.

"Is he okay?" I stepped into the yellow light peeking into the surrounding shadows. There, rusted beds filled with broken souls. Their eyes lifted to the ceilings as their lips dangled from their open mouths. "Holy shit."

Alexandre extended his long arms. The smile stretching across his face glowed beneath the yellowed light. "There's five more down here. You believe that?"

I looked at the machines pumping life into the money-making vegetables. "It's like its own senior center." Their half-open eyes were sunken back into their heads. "This is one of those old farms. You know, the ones Bruce was telling us about down at Victor's bar."

"You think so?"

I raised my hands toward the tired bodies glued to the beds surrounding us. "I don't think these people just walked down into this basement on their own."

Alexandre stepped over the creaking old man. "There's no way that kid from the pawnshop was working this thing alone?" He moved the curtains around, unveiling the workshop and the washer and dryer.

"Didn't Bruce mention something about there being cartel's running these things?"

An outside door slammed, shaking the warped floorboards in the kitchen. The handguns immediately raised from Alexandre's sides toward the stairs. Whoever that was, I'm sure they wouldn't be happy to see us.

"That shit better not be cold again, Mona," the man's voice called out. The chunky, rubber boots moved across the back steps.

Another moan lifted from the floor. Alexandre raised his finger to his lips, shushing the cries for help.

"Goddamnit is that Lenny, again?" the angry voice yelled as the spoon clanked against the bowl. "Pedro, I thought I told you to give him those damn meds. Do I have to put your asses in the hole until we learn the damn lesson?"

"My name is not Pedro," the old man called out. "It's Umberto."

"I'm thinking this ain't Cartel run," I whispered to Alexandre.

"I don't give a shit what your name is. I'm gonna be putting your ass down in that basement with the rest of those retards, and you're gonna be taking breakfast, lunch, and dinner down there for the next month if you don't start doing what I tell your ass."

Don't say we're here. Don't say we're here. Don't say we're here. Please, don't say we're here.

"Lenny's okay," the old woman's voice mentioned. "Ginny and Steve stopped by to help him out."

"Who the hell are Ginny and Steve?" the angered voice asked.

"That's my niece and nephew."

"Mona, you don't have no nieces or nephews," the man yelled. "You forget that shit, too?"

The boots continued toward the corner where I had seen the breakfast nook, prepped for supper.

"I'm telling you right now; we're cutting your fucking meds. Over here talking about imaginary people. Oh, and look at that, you burned the damn roux, AGAIN. You need to quit talking that crazy shit all the time and start worrying about your job around here before you find yourself out on the street."

The sound of the chair scraping against the kitchen floor echoed through the basement. The boots moved into the first bedroom. There was a pause as we listened just below the footsteps.

"I gotta go back out. I want this place spic and span when I get back," the angry voice called out. "Emphasis on the <u>spic</u>, Pedro. Quit watching so much God damn TV, you good for nothing sack of shit."

Dust from the floorboards above us dropped as the man stepped back into the kitchen. The sound of the boots stomping down each step thumped across the floor toward the back of the house.

I looked over at Alexander. He was ready to take on anything that came at us.

Suddenly the shitkickers, covered in reddened mud, appeared at the top of the basement steps. The backdoor opened. The breeze wafted the smell of the old man's leg into the air.

Alexander looked down at the uncomfortable old-timer, withering into the floor. "Shhhhhhhhhh."

Shots ripped through the base panels of the back door. Rounds tore up the folded stacks of linens and shattered the light just above our heads. Return fire from Alexander's pistols sent me diving under one of the beds.

I called to Alexander as the boots reappeared on the steps. The end of a rifle dangled at the rubber toes of the muddied boots. Rounds continued at random lighting up the basement.

"Alexandre," I shouted, watching his head drop to the floor in the faint light.

There was a pause. The silence set into the dark basement.

"I can hear you bitch," the voice called out. "Sounds like you and your little boyfriend done came into the wrong house today."

The boots marched down the creaky steps as I curled up under the nasty hospital bed.

"And would you look at that, damn it? You made me shoot Lenny," the voice said. "Sorry about that, old friend."

I watched as the round entered the forehead of the shaking man on the floor. Next to him laid Alexandre. Guns in hand, he was frozen to the ground from the spray. And I was next.

I could see the rubber-toed boots turn toward me. The white sheet on the old woman's bed above me lifted, revealing the tattered blue jeans.

"Well, hello there." The thick-bearded man with the broken teeth pointed the gun down at my face. "Say, I'm looking at your boyfriend over here, and I don't think he's gonna make it. So, now I guess I'm gonna have to kneecap your ass to replace what Lenny was bringing in. Hope you like seafood gumbo, bitch."

The blasts from across the basement floor sent pieces of the man's leg onto the floor next to me. His beard and face followed with an additional burst of birdshot. I was frozen stiff with the fury of the shotshells ringing in my ears. I jumped out from under the bed. The old woman from the kitchen at the top of the steps held the side-by-side in her wrinkled hands. The red shells exited the smoking barrels. "I don't burn roux."

I slipped on the soaked floor running for Alexander's side. "Just hold on," I yelled as his white shirt reddened. "We found our treasure; there's no way I'm letting you leave me now."

His bloodied smile drew tears from my eyes.

The old woman looked down at me from the steps, gun in

hand. "I'll ready the hole in the yard."

5

"I can't let you go outside today." Phil was unwinding the bear trap next to the front door. "You see those skies; it's gonna pour."

"I just wanna sit on the front porch for a little while," the old man said. "Mona lets me go out all the time."

Standing over the wheelchair, I could see the child-like testing rearing its head. "Now, what did I just say?"

The old man's shoulders slumped, wrinkling his coffee-stained t-shirt.

"Phil, when I come around, I expect you to listen. I know Mona doesn't let you out on that front porch when a God damn hurricane's headed this way. So I don't even wanna hear it."

Umberto waved me off. "Shit, that's just gonna be another tropical storm by the time it makes landfall." The two of them loved to try to work me over. "Let the man go outside. He's been in here, cooped up all week."

I noticed my finger wagging at them as any doting mother would. "Look. I can't afford you falling and breaking your hip on me, now can I?"

"But I just wanna go outside," Phil cried. "I might not see another storm like this again in my life."

Phil, you know damn well you've seen two of these things in the six years I've been in the picture. These old farts were driving me nuts. I usually tried to keep an even keel around them. They'd need an extra dose of blood pressure meds if I started getting pissed. We were bringing in good money on the BP meds on the street, so I had to watch what I said and how I said it.

"Phil, honey, I can assure you; you won't see another storm

like it in your life because if you step out that door, I'm gonna lock it behind you." I smiled at the testy old man speaking slow and easy. "And when those gale-force winds pick your old ass up in that rocking chair and set you down in a swamp somewhere, nobody's gonna be able to find you. Okay?"

The old man wavered next to the booby trap. I could see his hand shaking. He wanted to grab the handle on the mismatched beige paint of the repaired door. But he knew I wasn't playing games.

"You hear me, Phil? That means no more of Miss Mona's cooking. No more bridge, no more late nights with the boys. You step out that door, and I'm gonna let that storm just take you away."

Phil dropped his arms to his sides. The black hat with the yellow military bars fell over his face.

Steam from the hot chocolate in Mona's hands wafted into the living room air. "Phil, hon, go have a seat by the window. I'll fix you something warm, okay?"

His rickety hips popped as Phil folded back into the rusty wheelchair. Umberto chuckled. It was a small win but a win, regardless.

"That's much better." After the demands, I always followed up with praise. It was the only way I could get them to do what I needed and not lose the house. There were other farmers out there, and I needed to keep visibility as low as possible.

The melted chocolate bar in the steamed milk brought a smile to Phil's face. What would I do without Mona?

"Now, if we're all good," I continued, glaring at Phil. "This evening, I may get ice cream for everyone."

"I want Ms. Harris back!" Phil grumbled. "She was so nice."

Ms. Harris was our former in-home nurse. I paid her off-book to do the dirty work I'd been able to escape after the first year and a half of moving medications on the street through the D'or Demons. But when the insurance plans started cutting into me last year, I had to cut back.

"When is my Sally coming back?" Phil asked.

I winced at the question. Phil always got sentimental when he had hot chocolate. I should've told Mona to bring tea. "Sally's gone, Phil. She passed last year." I figured with the time passing that would somehow get easier to say. It didn't.

Phil slouched down in his chair and rubbed the chocolate from his nose. I could see him processing what I said. There was still light in his eyes. "Didn't you mention something about ice cream?" But where that light went exactly. I wasn't sure.

"I did, and I will get it." The guilt ate away my conscious. "I just need to check the basement, and I will go grab it."

Stepping out of the front sitting room, I caught a glimpse of the corner bed where Sally used to spend her days and nights. The hand-knitted afghans were still folded at the metal footboard.

I picked up speed before stopping to see Winston at the front of the beds. And there was that great big smile of his–complete with drool running down his chin.

"I don't know how you deal with these guys sometimes." I could see Mona's eyebrows were singed again. I tried to get rid of the match-lit gas stove. But after she fired a shot at the guys dropping off the electric range top, I gave up on the idea and prayed she didn't burn the house down.

Bursts of reddish-brown sauce blended into the woman's burgundy sweater. The loose fabric moved dangerously close to the blue flames of the old stove. It was how she'd done things since I'd been here, and she hadn't slowed. Who was I to tell her how to run her kitchen? All I could do was put up extra fire extinguishers and hope she didn't set herself on fire.

"Oh, Ginny, baby, you just gotta do it," Mona remarked, wooden spoon in hand. "They are people, just like you and me. They just sometimes–forget."

I grabbed the box of pills off the table and gloved up for the basement. The iodine smell remained at the back door as I made my way down the steps. The green glow from the monitors lit the floor as I made my rounds. The smell of rot exiting the open mouths filled my chest with a sense of comfort. Everyone was stable, and their diapers were clean. The original farm was still producing.

That same digital green reflected off the saline bags and feeding tubes as I gave them a flick. I looked over Derek and Danny. I didn't know their actual names, so that's what I called them for the past six years. Now it was time to check on the newbies. A heart attack and a blood clot left Mario and Luigi over here in full paralysis. There was no bickering, no movement, and no emotional outbursts in the basement. There was only the silence necessary to hear the machines feeding them just enough calories for their checks to keep cashing.

"I thank you, gentleman, for your service."

At the top of the steps, I snagged the cardboard box. Mona was starting the dinner service. She carefully pressed the craters into the rice mounds with her ladle. It left just enough space for the molten gumbo to overflow. That seemed like a lot of work to me. But she had a system.

The sparkle from my ring caught her eye as I ungloved and took off the white jacket. The pink tassels from my jacket bounced down the open-chested blazer I had just bought.

Mona gave me a toothy smile. "Well, now, don't you look nice."

I removed the old rubber-toed boots and put my heels back on. "Somebody's gotta keep those stewpots of yours filled." I smiled at the lovely woman with the warm, inviting face. "I just wish the cost of shrimp would go down some."

I looked at the woman who saved my life all those years back. She hadn't changed one bit. Her eyes were just as blue-gray as they were when I first walked into that house. And those wrinkled hands of hers were just as strong.

I heaved the box of pills out the back door. "I'll see you tomorrow afternoon."

"Sounds good, baby." Mona stayed focused on dinner. The ladle filled each bowl exactly the same.

Phil and Umberto were peeking into the kitchen.

"Don't take any of that crap off those two."

The overcast skies brought a gust of cool wind. There was

something cooking up there. A loud knocking erupted from the fenced-in backyard. The sound startled me, causing me to lose my grip on the box.

I hadn't looked in the yard since that first day on my old farm. I hadn't done a lot of things I used to before that day. I pulled the pistol out of my pocket and moved toward the loud slamming. If it was one of those sick freaks, I was gonna make sure they knew this was not the place to mess with.

"Hello over there." I marched toward the rundown house next door. "I've got a little something for you. Come on out. I won't bite."

The slamming grew louder as I closed in on the back of the house. There was still nothing. Either they were really patient, or I was losing it. Even with the gun, I had to build up some nerve to turn that corner.

A dangling piece of siding on the overgrown house next door rattled against the plywood, covering the window. The hunk of metal the junkies couldn't reach for scrap echoed through the neighborhood.

I'd been out of the game for far too long.

I took a deep breath, put my gun away, and moved down the alley. Clinging to the box of cylindrical gold, I climbed into the safety of the pink and gold SUV. There I unleashed the breath I'd been holding.

The dark corner of the backyard where the aluminum siding banged away, called to me. I couldn't believe it had been as long as it had been. Staring the engine, I fought looking back.

A quick breath, and I pulled away toward the new life I'd made.

6

The bold blue of the spatulas slid an assortment of pinks, whites, yellows, and reds across the slick plastic. My crew of mixed teenagers, naked from the chest up, moved in a constant flow. It was a system perfected over the last five and a half odd years. We were not the only game in town, but my people had their shit together.

"And how are we doing today, Sophie?"

Sophie hopped up from the long plywood table. "The scales are moving things along much faster Ms. Renee."

"Good, I don't wanna hear any bitching from the doctors this time. They get what I give them. And if those punk-ass D'or Demons have any other complaints, then they can come and talk to our friend upstairs."

I looked over the fluorescent lighting. The hired hands moved like coked-up craps dealers, shuffling buy-ins down the line.

"One for you, two for me, one for you two for me," the counter with the thin beard repeated. His quick fingers slid orange vials across the table into waiting boxes.

"Hey Franco," I called out. "What's the count looking like?"

"One for you, two for me, one for you--"

"Franco!"

"What?" he yelled. He stopped and looked up to see it was his boss. "Oh, sorry, Ms. Renee."

"The count?"

"If we go on the streets, it looks like we'd be at four-hundred for the week."

Boots echoed, coming down the steps. "That's IF those

fucking doctors cooperate. They said they didn't want these any-more." The overflowing box of vials dropped on the table from the hands of my distribution head. "Some bullshit about some bad side effects. If we wholesale to the doctors, we'd be looking at maybe two."

The other farmers were catching on. I knew it was a matter of time before the market got saturated. We had a niche, working the door-to-door delivery service for a while there. But even in broad daylight, loads were getting hit. "Then you go out, and you give them to the Demons, Marty. They can sell them to the junkies and those plague-ridden monsters. They don't have a problem with side effects."

"That's fine," Marty said, "but I'm not doing another shoot-out with those motherfuckers on Frenchman."

"Take them over to Canal. I've been doing business with those guys since I started. You shouldn't have any problems in there."

"Yeah, you said that about the guys on Frenchman. And I lost Dylan, Sammy, and Max to the crew that spots for Vick the Dick's place."

Distribution wasn't going quite as smooth, which is why I had to recruit added firepower. "And that is why I told you to stay away from Victor's. That's also why I paid for the turret last year just in case anything like that happened again. So I don't wanna hear it."

Marty rolled his eyes, leaning against the hand-cut stone walls. He was getting more and more insubordinate. With the bigger deals slipping, I had the feeling he was looking for work elsewhere.

I stepped into his face and pressed my finger to his chest. "That thing cost me an arm and a leg. And the only reason I did that was so if you ever got into trouble, you'd have something to fall back on." The guilt dropped his eyes. "So quit bitching."

Really, I put that turret in place, so if I ever got into trouble, I would have something to fall back on. But Marty didn't need to know that. Thinking it was for his benefit gave him the warm fuzzy feeling the advanced weapon system provided. And it allowed me to sleep at night.

I needed to find a replacement for Marty. He was losing his nerve. He was starting to get shaky on the deals, and his returns were less and less every other week. Even before the insurance companies changed tactics, I noticed money starting to trail off on his runs. He didn't look sick, but he also wasn't in here with his shirt off anymore. I graduated him off the tables and onto the street because he seemed to have the temperament for it. But it looks like I may've been wrong.

"Just make it happen, folks," I told them. "I had a long afternoon–and oh shit, I forgot the ice cream."

"Ice cream?" Marty asked.

Damn it, Phil. You had to ask the second time. That meant Humberto wasn't gonna forget. And they were gonna piss and moan next time I was there if I didn't bring it over.

"You want me to--"

"No!" I cut Marty off. "I'll take care of it."

Marty had been trying to get a lock on the locations of my farms for months. Nobody ever knew where the pills came from. I had to keep that secret under lock and key. If they ever found out, they wouldn't need me anymore.

There's no telling what the drones would do if they got into the hives. This is why I kept private drivers, private doctors, and in-house nurses separate from the drugs at all times. The additional costs were well worth the restful sleep. My people were just as bad as any one of those monsters I dealt to. They would use any angle to take all my hard work away from me. I'd never make it easy for them, but there was always the chance I'd wake up with my throat cut.

Profits were receding. It was only a matter of time before I would have to make a move. I had to figure out a new way to make these farms work for me.

7

"I had this all planned out. We were supposed to escape. It was supposed to be the two of us when we finally hit it. If you could see the car I'm in, the clothes I'm wearing, and the house I live in now, you'd be so proud. You'd be right here with me; you know that. You could've gone back home and just thrown all that money around. Bought your mom out of that shack she lived in. Bury those brothers and sisters in drinks and drugs until they were so wasted and jealous they wouldn't be able to see straight. My mom wouldn't give a shit, but yours would've been so proud. My dad, he would've loved this. It would've been so great... had you just gotten to see it."

I stared at the back corner of the yard from the comfort of the spacious SUV. A half pack of cigarettes disappeared in what seemed like seconds. I looked over the faded gingerbread somebody very proud carved and added to the front porch of the old house, my house. One of many I had stuffed to the gills with walking, talking money bags. MY walking, talking money bags.

"Shit!" The gigantic, see-through plastic ice cream bucket was melting. The protective ice layer was leaking all over my leather seat--the things I did for my flock.

The inside of the house was like the old casino before the river took it in the last flood. Time stood still in there. If I didn't know Mona had already served dinner, I wouldn't think anything changed since the last time I was here.

White velcro strapped shoes were lined-up in the same spot in the kitchen. Jackets and knit hats were right where whoever used them last had left them. I put on the doctor's coat and the thick boots and started for the front room. The bucket of ice cream dangled from my hand.

The smell lingered from the mashup of vegetables and seafood as it always did. If I could turn Mona's cooking into a restaurant, the stew she made would've paid off my house faster than the pills. But that was another life. One I'd never touch. And really, one I had no interest in.

A TV flickered in the middle room. Their eyes locked in on the bucket of cheap vanilla ice cream.

"Hey, somebody remembered," Humberto poked, behind the silver mustache.

"Can you please try to keep it down?" I could hear the agitation in Mona's voice from the front room even before she turned the corner. "I just got Phil to sleep."

I rolled my eyes. "Phil's asleep? I went to two stores to get him his ice cream."

"That was nice of you, Ginny. But you know how he gets around sundown." I could see the taxation in Mona's eyes from Phil's fit.

I'd seen Phil weep and scream like a child around the time the shadows set in on the front porch. It was bizarre. He was a different person for an hour, and then he'd finally calm down when the sun set. The only other place I'd seen that was on the street, back when we were working the Quarter.

We'd see the SIL junkies traveling in packs around the same time every day. It was around that time we knew to find a place to hide.

Shadows would grace the window sills of abandoned buildings during the day. Inside, you'd hear them stirring. Occasionally, I would see a random loner on the streets in the sunlight. But it was right around sunup and sunrise when they'd make their raids.

When we did stick-ups, Alexandre and I would find shelter when the sun would rise and set. Time was something I was told never existed in the Quarter before the storms and the plague. Now time was on the minds of everyone who stepped into the streets.

"It's been worse with Phil since Sally left us," Mona added.

The spoons as I set the bucket of melting ice cream down on the TV dinner table. Humberto dove right in.

"I gotta get back." I marched past Mona toward the kitchen. Everything was in its place. "Just make sure Phil gets some of this."

I turned back to see Mona, standing in the doorway with her hands in her pockets. "I will, dear. You don't worry about us. We're just fine here."

I locked the back door and avoided the backyard. I noticed the sound of the loose siding was gone. I sprinted through the alley. Inside the SUV, I took a deep breath and started the drive back toward civilization.

Moving down Humanity Avenue, I saw the faint lights inside my other farms. Places where I rescued the elderly and put them up rent-free. Places where they could live and have whatever they needed. And it was all on me, all of it. I took care of them, so I got to choose who stayed and who went. So fuck you, Phil. It was Sally's time to go. Get over it. You're starting to be more of a fuss than you're worth. Maybe I should just send your ass packing, too.

The glow of the city up ahead took me out of the sprawl of the suburban dead zone. Thank God.

Those people should be kissing my feet after everything I'd done for them. But enough about them. I was finally off the clock. This is my time now.

My polished ride moved through the wreckage of the SIL-infested streets. A feeling of ease lifted over my anxiety as I hit the first row of mansions where in my neighborhood. "Get me the two-combo," I called out. The car returned with the confirmation of my order. Pulling up to the gates of my house, I looked at the ivy climbing up the powder blue siding toward the turret. It hadn't all come back yet since the renovations. But it would come back.

The lights were off in the basement. I could just make out

the little red light on in the turret. If people only knew what was in that thing, maybe they'd pick another street to walk down. After what it cost me, I was almost afraid to use the thing. But if these punks keep coming around throwing trash in my yard, somebody's getting lit up.

I put a shoulder into the huge front door. I could hear the sound of the frame stretch. You know, when you pay what I did for a house, I felt like they should update everything. And that included the God damn doors that stuck in the summer heat. I waved and smiled at the neighbors, just making out their faces over my wall. They were sitting down to their morning coffee and didn't wave back. They must not've seen me.

Stepping through the parlor, I could smell the cutting agent Franco had been experimenting with. The chemical aroma seeped up from the basement.

"Were these assholes born in a barn?"

I unlocked the deadbolt, securing the cage separating the basement from the rest of the house. Looking down into the darkened basement, I couldn't hear anything. There were creaks in the house and basement. And I had pinpointed all of them. But shutting the place down for the night still gave me the jeebies. So, I pulled the .380 from my purse just to be safe as I locked up the deadbolt. I knew damn well if I found a way into this place, others could too.

I stepped back into the same house I once wandered into as a lowly pro working on Madam Honeydew's shit list and looked around. My ceilings were tall in the main lobby, like a bank or a hotel. My rounded stairs lead up to a balcony. I tried to have my house filled by one of the local furniture stores. But they were asking for my firstborn for a set of couches. So, I just snagged what I needed for me, including my king-sized bed, and called it a day. Hey, if people wanna come over, they can sit on the floor. It's more expensive than anything they've probably ever parked their asses on, anyway.

My heels clanked off the marble as I moved toward the balcony. At the top of the steps, rather than the comfort of the master suite, I made a left toward the front of the house. I opened the wooden door and sealed the hatch behind me.

"Ahhhhh." It was like the safety just streamed right out of my chest. The turret doubled as a safe room, as well as my last line of defense. The metal, which normally would be icy to the touch, was heated by the rising afternoon temperatures. It was warm compared to the rest of the air condition house. But it was a good heat.

I sat down in the chair and looked down the sights of my death machine. And to think, this whole thing, all this protection, just cost me one comatose old lady. I closed my eyes and leaned into the weaponry. The jagged corners delivered the feeling of safety. It was just what I needed right then and there.

I opened my eyes and saw the delivery driver. Looking at the front end of the champagne SUV, I wondered what this thing could do if I_just_pressed_this_button. I see the number two combo and take a deep breath before stepping out of the warmth of safety.

The call from the gate echoed through the house.

"Let them in," I told the security system.

A quick jerk, and there, at my front door stood the hooded couple. The light from my chandelier exposed their faces. Their brown eyes lightened the heaviness in my chest. First shift.

The farms were closed. The equipment had all been put away. And my work was done for the day. Looking over their taut skin, I felt young again.

8

All those years of caring for my herd and with a swipe of a pen, it was all over.

We regret to inform you we will be cutting your medical benefits effective immediately. Medications will now be paid out of pocket. Treatments and Doctor visits will require a fifty dollar co-pay and your deductible for the year will be ten-thousand-five-hundred-and-fifty-dollars. If you have any problems with the change in plan, please let us know. We are here to help. This is a trying time for our community as we continue the fight against SIL. We are aware there will be a lot of upset people out there, and we are here to help in any way we can.
All the best,
Joseph P. Allinger
Governor

The stack of nearly two hundred letters spilled across my leopard sheets. Ten houses, each filled six years worth of livestock, and they were being called in for the slaughter. Why would they do this to these people? They never hurt anyone.

It was only a matter of time before the wolves would start sniffing. The gangs, the doctors, the system, they would all have leverage on me again. They could take it all away.

I stepped out of bed and grabbed some leftover favors from my order. My head felt like it dragged down the hallway as I moved along the balcony. My eyes searched over the massive house, once owned by one of the business royalty of New Orleans. I looked at the endless open floors. I looked at all the money I put into the security, logistics, and even what little furniture I had. I looked over at the turret. All I wanted to do was unleash that beast on the rest of these tight-ass neighbors; I knew they saw me when I waved. Shit, I'd bet that couple next door probably put that governor up to this insurance grab just to get me out of here. Who was I kidding? These people would never accept me. And now I was gonna have to sell this place.

A jolt from the brownish powder Franco had created, and I was back in the game. Woah! Leaning over the carved railing, I looked down onto my dynasty. Everything I made. ME. And now it was all going to be taken.

Another bump widened my eyes. I could feel the secret recipe of pharmaceutical leftovers light up my insides. What the hell was in this?

There was no way fucking I was gonna go out that easy. I'd burn this place to the ground before I'd sell it. There's no way I was gonna let some little pussy governor, who'd sucked his way into power, take everything I did away from me. I beat street gangs; I beat doctors; I beat their stupid bull-shit system. And I did it all by myself. There was no way I was letting that all go--Not after the price I paid to get here. Fuck that.

I had lost Alexander. I had broken my back mining those old bastards. I'd put together contacts with doctors and made nice with every low-life drug dealer in town.

I took a seat, allowing my heart to catch up to whatever Franco put in his mix. I could feel every last inch of rage in my system shaking in my fists. Whatever this was, it was strong. I tried to take a breath as the high continued.

There was no chance I was gonna just give that up.

"You are all late!" My crew of misfits stumbled down the basement stairs. I could smell the liquor pouring from their skin. They looked like hammered-shit. By the smell of them, they'd been on Bourbon Street.

Marty wiped the morning from his bloodshot eyes. "Damn, who the fuck are you down here in the dungeon up all early and shit?"

I needed their full attention. "This is who the fuck I am." I pulled the handgun from my purse and slammed it on the metal table. "We are going to be diversifying our business."

Their eyes all stayed with the pistol.

"I'm sure many of you know this already, but things have not been going as well around here as I would like. The pills have not been bringing the returns I want. So, changes are necessary. Your heads are all on the block with the future of this business. Because after all, how am I going to be able to pay you without a return on our little project here."

I could see the fear in the few who actually needed the job. Then there was a smile from the self-starters, like Marty, who wanted my head.

"Now, you're not out yet. I would like to keep every last one of you on. I want things to go back to the way they were--When the money was pouring in. I know you have mouths to feed and ridiculous things to buy. So, me being the gracious boss I am, will be liquidating assets to keep the lot of you on as contract workers."

Their faded eyes looked at me with confusion. I hadn't lost them, which meant I still had their attention.

"Which means no more cushy salaries. You will be paid according to your output."

The news was settling into their faces. It's not that they didn't work. Not a single one of them was lazy. They performed every task I asked of them. But they were now going to have to stretch themselves from the drone work to the challenge of coming up with new business ventures.

"Thanks to some flapjack-assed politician, our pill supply will be dwindling. So we are going to be grinding out what we have left and starting over."

"I don't know about all of this." A frazzled Franco stepped toward the table. Under his hand was the bag filled with the concoction. The same stuff that nearly blew my heart from my chest earlier in the morning. "This mix has been gaining some ground out there. Did you try that new shit I made from the reds and the yellows?"

I stared into the gangly teenager. The new drug he called "Rabbit" surged through my veins. "What about there will be no more pills, do you not understand. Our supply's been cut off." I looked down at the box of orange vials I took from my first farm yesterday. "This is all I have left."

"That's okay. I can work with that," Franco said. "If you can give me those and what we have left of those leftovers from yesterday, I can get five times what we were getting with my mixture."

Franco had become an artist. With only a high school diploma, he could put down any lab rat in the city, making more in a day's worth of work than any of them could in a year. He'd used the hand he'd been dealt and had played it masterfully. It was high time I did the same. "That's fine and dandy, but we are still gonna be out of pills by the end of the month. Unless...."

I could see the gears turning in Marty's head. He knew something. He leaned into the metal table, staring at the pistol. "Unless what?" The fluorescent overhead lighting created long shadows under his brow as he stared into me.

"You just leave that to me. And as for the rest of you, unless you wanna be working for Madam Honeydew, slinging your ass, I would expect some forward movement."

9

The phone on my desk was warm to the touch. The screen was covered in sweat and grease from the drive-thru breakfast I stuffed down. "Yes, my houses on Roman, Egania, Choctaw, and Villere, along with all the equipment inside, are yours," I said calmly. My farms were drying up. I had little choice left. They were all being sold to a new owner. "And for that price, I require cash, upfront, and at my house, delivered by you."

"No, no checks, no runners, no delivery men. I want to meet you. I've been responsible for these people's personal care for a long time. I need to meet who I'm going to be selling my family to. Right, and I'm still kicking myself for that deal. I should've never let Sally go to you. But we all have to do what we have to do. I just want to make sure you keep your end of the bargain. You have to bring her back to be with her husband."

The desk was covered with the rest of the rabbit mix Franco put together for me. I'd been ripping at the dust all morning to keep the little conscious I had left buried and the deals moving.

My office door burst open, sending my hand for the gun on the desk. "You know I almost shot your ass."

"No need," Marty said, grabbing his left arm in pain. "Those motherfuckers down on Frenchman grazed me as I walked out the door."

"Did they take the deal?"

"Yeah, fuck you, too."

"Here." I passed him a hit of the rabbit.

He took a bump of Franco's finest, and his eyes nearly blew out of his head. "Yeah, they took it. They said they'd be here around 7:30." I noticed the grip on the wound loosening.

"There are no abouts with this thing. I need them here at 7:30. You tell them, they are either here at 7:30 with the pills or the deal is off."

"I don't know why you think this thing is gonna work," Marty said, letting go of the bullet wound. "Once they see you got Silver Savages out there, they are gonna be wondering what the fuck is up."

"Right." I swiped the drip from my nose. "Then the blood will be in the water. And they may just wipe themselves out for us."

Marty looked back at me. His pupils were pinpoint. "And if not?"

"Well, then we're gonna have to supply a little pressure to stir things up."

Marty pulled the gun out of his pocket and set it down on the desk. Blood from the wound had found its way into the chamber.

"What the hell are you doing with that?"

"What do you think?" He glared at the chunk missing out of his arm. "It's nuts out there."

"No, no, no, no, no. No guns. We have to be completely clean inside the house. No pills, no guns, no blood trails, nothing. This place has to spotless."

"Shit, you got one," he said, pointing at my loaded .380.

"That's right, I do." I slid the pistol across the desk. "And I want you to take this and any other contraband the others might have down to Mickey's. He'll beat you up on the price, but you sell it, all of it. This house has to be immaculate. We need to pretend like we belong here, so if we do face questioning, we are just members of the neighborhood who work in the retirement business."

I watched Marty staring into the lamp on my desk. "Did you hear me?" My heart exploded from my chest. Jesus Christ, what did Franco put in this?

"Yeah." His eyes were donuts, glazed front to back.

"Well, then?"

Rising from the chair, he grabbed the guns off the desk. He stared down at me with a pistol in each hand. It was there; I saw it. But I also saw the hesitation. He may've wanted to, but he didn't have the balls to pull the trigger on me.

He tucked the guns into his waistband. Heading for the door, the wad of bills I tossed smacked down on the floor next to him.

"Go down to Decatur. There's a place with a reddish-orange roof. A doctor lives there. His name is Manopolous. Have him look at that arm. Tell him Renee and Alexander sent you. And if that doesn't jog his memory, show him the cash."

Marty snagged the money. I could hear him clip-clopping down the staircase.

"Negotiate the price," I yelled with a smile. "Keep some of that for your time! You earned it."

I leaned back in the chair and bumped more rabbit. This was going to work.

10

Sundown. The darkness crept into my beautiful neighborhood. Lights from the overpriced vehicles filled with crazed street thugs shined in the warm, foggy night air. The chippy attitudes and firearms began revealing themselves in the street out in front of the gate of my mansion.

There, at the cast-iron gate, the lone real estate broker with the low-cut goatee stood waiting. He was the one I sold Sally to when times were tight last year. And he was now the one I brokered a deal selling off the rest of my stock. The monitors in my office filmed every anxious tick on the man's face. Each check of his watch came with another car filled with the kind of gen pop psychos who'd eat the white-collar criminal for breakfast. Behind him, rival dealers from around the Quarter looked on. Engines revved in the street as they all flexed.

People I helped make were here to break me. They wanted everything I owned at a fraction of the cost. The real estate agent with the leather briefcase filled with cash took notice of the shit storm brewing behind him. I laughed, watching his finger reach out for my call button over and over again.

Inside the house, all of my workers were dressed to the nines. They'd brought plus ones and twos and threes to fill the banquet room. Music from the cotillion style ball roared, covering up the sound of the ringing doorbell.

A screech and a flash of headlights ripped down the street. The gang leaders jumped out of their cars.

Bursts of light exploded into the silence of the upscale neighborhood. The real estate agent ran for the safety of his truck. In a flash of controlled violence, the street was swept clean of all my rivals.

The black sedan decoy returned from the quick trip down the block. I watched along from behind the smoking turret as Marty and his team moved through the stew of carnage. Marty and my chemistry club picked salable items, including jewelry, guns, shoes, and jackets, clean from the carcasses. I could see the briefcase falling into the trunk of the car as my hooded soldiers moved quickly and quietly.

Inside the party of paid attendees gorged themselves on Franco's rabbit. They drained the house of even the faintest trace of pharmaceutical residue. Even if the music wasn't loud enough, I don't think the drug-induced trances would've let them hear what was happening outside.

I stepped out of the comfort of my office to the sounds of sirens. A quick touch up on the bags under my eyes, and I strolled into the party. The ring at my gate took me to the door. I could already see the cleanup teams moving over the bodies. They quickly dispatched any trace of the city's reality from the neighborhood.

"Hello, officers," I greeted with a smile. "How can I help you this evening?"

"Ma'am, were you aware there was an incident in front of your house this evening?"

11

An incident? Was he kidding? This wasn't just any <u>incident</u>. This was <u>my</u> incident. And it was playing out better than I had planned. Now I just needed the rabbit to loosen its legs for five while I sweet-talked these two bruisers out of here.

"No officer, I'm sorry. I've been hosting guests inside my home this entire evening." The dress, the makeup, the eyedrops, and the address; they all ensured I wouldn't see the inside of cuffs or even their car. There would be no rough stuff and no planted evidence. Even if those dusty cunts from next door said I had anything to do with this, I would be sleeping in my own bed tonight.

"Do you mind if we take a look around?"

"Not at all, Claude, can you turn the music down a bit, please? These officers want to take a look around. Reginald, can you take everyone into the kitchen for a bite? I think they need to have a look at the street. Apparently, there was an incident out in front."

"Heavens to Betsy!" Clive, one of my runners, said, waving people into the dining room. "Don't you worry about a thing Miss Renee, I will make sure the quiche is ready for service."

They were better actors than they were chemists. Because let's be honest, Franco was the brains behind rabbit.

"Ma'am, if you don't mind, we need to get a look from the front of the house–upstairs."

The officers began their search through my mansion. They searched and searched and searched. They may not've been buying the mumsy routine, but they had a better chance of finding Jimmy Hoffa than any trace of evidence linking me to the chaos on the street.

Approaching the door to the turret, the last hit of the rabbit began to make me sweat some. Holy shit, let's just hope selling Sally was going to pay off.

The lady cop's hand slowly turned the knob. I could see the tension in her body as she braced for impact.

A crack in the door revealed the open hardwood floors. Bright lights from the street poured in the window of the empty octagonal room.

The officer looked over the bare plaster walls. "Not much furniture in this house. You just move in?"

"Well, we try to keep it light and airy. Anything you get these days has the possibility of getting ripped off by those SIL junkies, and we don't like to attract a lot of attention to ourselves."

The glare from the cleanup crew in the streets cast a shadow on the officer standing at the window. He looked into the tarped mess now walled off from the sight of the neighborhood.

"Well, you just let us take care of that ma'am," the lady cop said. "You have nothing to worry about around here. We've done our best to keep those monsters out of this neighborhood, and we will continue to do so."

The broad-shouldered policeman smiled at me. "We'll get this whole thing cleaned up, lickety-split."

The cops and I both knew those SIL junkies were attracted to gunshots. I could remember back in the Quarter; they were like magnets to violence. Anything they could snag or steal was something more than they had before. And that was exactly why I instructed Marty to make the hit look like the infected outsiders beat them to the scene. With the turret tucked away under the floorboards, my people would be able to maintain the party while I counted the haul in the basement.

I held back the laughter and joy the rabbit wanted so badly to unleash in front of the cops. "Well, we sure are thankful for all that you do for us."

The lead officer stepped away from the window. "We are very sorry we interrupted your party."

The broad-shouldered bloodhound who had been searching the walls finally turned off her nose. "Again, we don't want you or your guests to worry. We will have what's left of this mess cleaned up by the end of your evening, and we can get everyone home safe."

"We are truly sorry for the disturbance," the woman said. "If you have any problems or see anyone who looks out of place on the street, please give us a call."

I took the card from the man's immense hand. Around here we paid by the pound for our police. The bigger, the better. "Thank you very much; I will do that if I see anything."

The female officer continued to look me over. She still had her questions. But they would never be asked. All thanks to my beautiful powder blue house.

One last pull from the drugs brought the smirk to my face as I closed the door behind them. "Good night."

12

The back door of the run-down shack up off Burk had the one smell that could bring a morning's worth of sausage, egg, croissants back into this world. I slid the bloodied keys from the real estate agent into the door. That salty sewage aroma brought me to a halt at the back of the house. The anti-nausea meds in the rabbit mix kept me together, thank God. But the odor brought tears to my eyes.

"What's that smell?" Marty asked.

"It's roses and perfume." I joked. "It's floodwater and garbage. What do you think it is?"

Marty pulled his shirt over his nose and mouth in disgust. "How the hell do you know that?"

"You brought the gun, right?"

"You told me to get rid of everything."

Pressing my eyes closed, I fought the urge to strangle my dumbass underling. I didn't know if the real estate agent had guards who were as handy with a 12-gauge as Mona or not. Either way, the rabbit was steering the ship, and I couldn't feel much from the neck down. "Just shut up and follow me."

No boots, no lab coat, and no gloves. I was entering the hellish living standards of the real-estate agent's farm with no protection. My dress and shawl were fresh from the faux ball. My plans to use the party as a cover to slaughter a slew of other dealers and farmers had given me the keys to a kingdom no politician could ever touch. But the crown sat heavily on my head. I needed to fix a mistake I'd made before I laid my claim to this throne.

Opening the door, I begged for the smell of seafood stew cooking. And I would've shoved mothballs up my nose to cover up the stench of whatever died in the house. Some farmers were smart, and they didn't have basements because of the floods. But knowing what that asshole was trying to get off me and for the price, I'm sure he had maximum storage space in his farms. And from the smell of it, he was saving money on the cleaning service.

The pair of beds in the kitchen breakfast nook set a precedent. Digital green flashed on the floors, as the gray-haired ghouls withered into their beds. There were more bed-ridden people stuffed into this house than in all of my places put together.

Any inch of space not covered in beds was overrun with diapers and empty fluid bags. I stepped through the field of humanity with the flashlight. Soiled underpads and empty orange vials littered the living room. Age made faces look very similar. Grayed and malnourished, unable to speak. The life sucked from their bones. It was a great business tactic, but looking into their faces, I could barely tell them apart.

It was at that moment I was so grateful for Mona. Without her, I would've never been able to start this business. I couldn't do this to people. They were someone's parents, someone's children. I had a conscience for God's sake.

The crazed woman in the front room screamed in a room of comatose stock. She saw me and squawked about the remote for the TV that wasn't working. Taking a close look at the television, I could see a range of bullet holes on the screen.

Marty swung the light over the drooping faces. "This place is nasty. What the hell are we doing here?"

Half living bodies, warped by time and potent medication, lined every last wall of the single level house. A search of the first floor and there was nothing. I really didn't want to go down in that basement.

The roaches took cover under browned sheets, and yellowed plastic bedpans as the flashlight hit the floor. "We gotta go down to the basement."

"Fuck that," Marty said. "I got no gun, and I don't even know why the fuck it is we're in here."

"Hey, you wanna get paid or not?"

I could see him searching over the orange pill vials. I was hoping he wasn't putting it all together. The fact was I found a way to the top not through the pill bottles or secrets of pharmacology, but as an old farmer. Yeah, I stumbled onto a fortune, but I made my strides in rubber boots one dirty diaper at a time.

"Damn it." Marty stepped toward the back door. He didn't want to go. But he knew there was a reason I was there, and he wanted to find out. "Fine."

Leading the way to the basement pen, I noticed my pumps, slathered in the brown sludge. I looked under the stairwell overhang. The aroma coming from around the door brought those tears right back to my eyes as I looked into the sea of beds. Jesus, what the hell did I do?

The stairs creaked under my feet as Marty followed behind. The smell was unbearable. Rusted hospital beds stacked up as far as the eye could see. As much as I wanted to turn away, I had to hold it together in front of my minion.

An inch or so of water, (or at least that's what I told myself the liquid on the floor was) sat on the cracked concrete. I started running the flashlight over the faces. They all had the same look. Their mouths were empty caverns. They had no teeth and no control of their lips or facial muscles. Their eyes hid in the back of their heads.

The flashlight moved over the faces, crossing ethnic borders. A white sheet dangled from a bed behind the furnace. Shuffling through the tight alleys, I kept my light on that sheet. The floor sloshed under my feet, but I heard nothing. I just maintained the glow and marched forward.

There, in the shit soaked herd of old, was the flowing, unkempt hair of Miss Sally. I took a deep breath of the sewage-stained air and nearly lost it.

"Let's go," I said, wiping my eyes. "Here she is!"

Marty's flashlight paused on the old woman's face. His puzzled look kept my confidence. He hadn't figured it out. And that was a good thing. The look of disgust and his hand over his mouth showed me the insanity of it all still blinded him. Little did he know the power the farm yielded when correctly used.

The weight came crashing from my shoulders. Grabbing either side of the sheet, we lifted Sally out of that misery.

I took Sally to my house first to clean off the residue of that awful basement pen.

I never had one of my old folks in my house. It was strange. These people helped build an empire, but never tasted the fruits it gave.

A confused Marty looked on in confusion. "Is she like your Grandma or something?"

"She is like my grandma or something," I told him. "Now, help me get her in the shower."

Cleaning her top to toe was nothing different for me. Marty stepped away at the sight of the wrinkles, and the liver spots.

"If you're gonna just stand there, you might as well go take all that stuff out of the back of your car and put it in my trunk."

Marty cut his eye at me before stepping out of the bathroom.

"All of it!"

When I got started, bathing was a job I did almost every other day with Mona. It took me a second to get used to the sponge baths, but after a while, it was just skin, bone, and profit. Keeping sores clean and bugs at bay kept pesky doctor visits and copays low.

Hosing off the brown tint from her frail skin brought me nearly to tears. I couldn't believe someone would do that to another human being.

I put her in one of the black dresses I didn't wear anymore and wheeled her into the main hall. It was strange; it almost felt like she should've been living there as opposed to me. Her skin tone and gaunt look in that black dress fit the era and style of the old house much better than the fluorescent pinks and vibrant yellows I regularly wore.

But it was me who created this empire. And that poor old woman wouldn't be sitting in this place without me. I looked around the mansion and felt a sense of pride swim over me.

13

Bringing Sally in the back door was no easy task by myself. But that sweet smell of stew and mothballs, along with a little help from Mona, helped me get her up and over the hump. My heart pounded, moving through the barrels of the old shotgun house. The nearly dead weight and the anticipation of seeing Phil's face when he saw the wife he thought was dead and gone was blowing my chest through my blouse.

We stopped in the middle room. With a heave, we put a cleaned up Sally in the black designer dress, back in her bed. I think I could almost see a smile cross her face as I stepped toward the front room. There, the boys were watching TV.

"Hey, Phil," I huffed. "I got a little surprise for you."

"You get any more of that ice cream?" Umberto asked.

"No," I returned, catching my breath. "But can you come in here for a second? I think it'll be something you might like."

"If it's not ice cream, I'm not interested."

"Phil," I returned calmly. "Can you please just come over here?"

The old man began wheeling himself over toward the doorway. "All right, all right." The anticipation was killing me. He was finally going to be reunited with his wife. And after all that planning, I would have that cake and could eat it too.

The old man stepped into the room with a flat look on his face. He looked over at me, emotionless.

"Who's that?" he asked.

"Phil, it's Sally."

"Who's Sally?"

My malfunctioning gate brought me into the warm night. The street in front of my house was cleansed of all my local competition. In just a few seconds, my turret put more money and more farms in my pocket than I had amassed in the six years since I started. The police had done a miraculous job in a short amount of time. But that was why I paid my taxes.

The light of day crept into the morning. I could see only traces of the kitty litter they used to soak up fluids from the shootout.

Birds chirped, and the smell of the blooming zinnias filled my lungs. I loved this neighborhood. I could see myself here, pruning a garden or whatever it is these people do for many years to come.

Looking down the street, I could see a man in a hoodie running toward me.

"Out for an early jog?" I asked with a smile. The blister ridden arms radiated in the red light of the emerging day. It was then, in the morning dew, I could feel the blade drive into my back.

MORE INFECTED

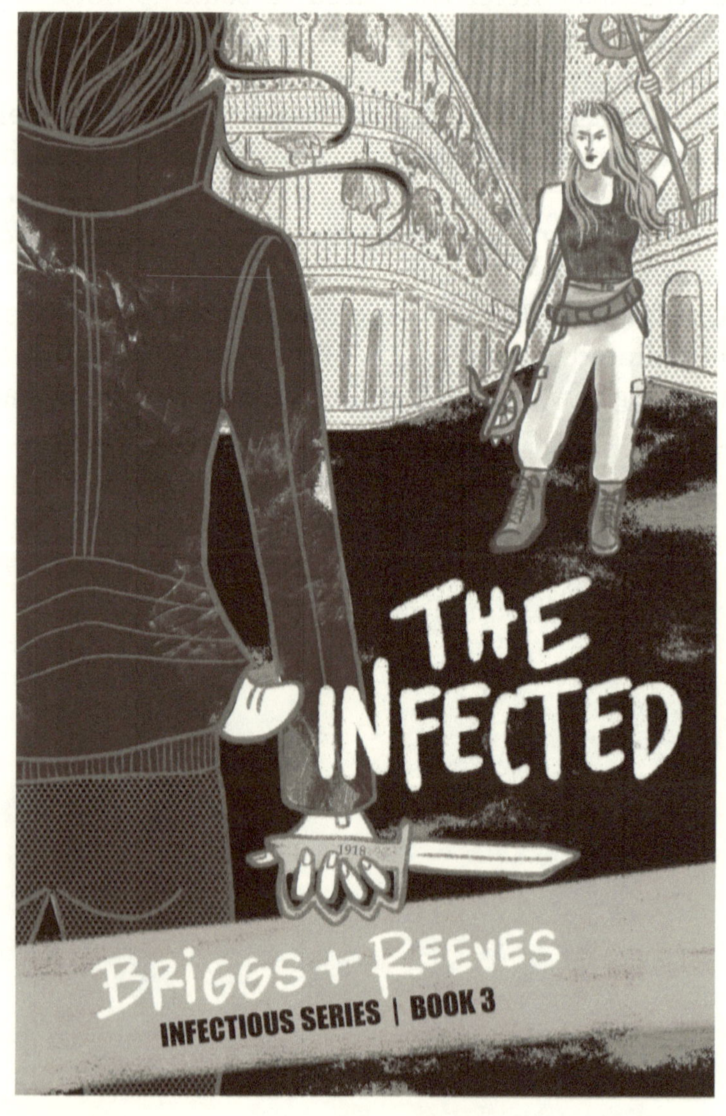

Go underground with legions of the diseased in

Part 3 of the Infectious Series, THE INFECTED

COMING SOON FROM BRIGGS AND REEVES!
www.briggsandreeves.com

BOOKS BY THIS AUTHOR

The Feed

"A study conducted by one of our followers has shown Feed is addicting. With any luck, we could be the next cigarettes."
In a small zoo in silicon valley, revolution is at hand. The human race has left the planet in shambles, and now it's up to the animals to save the world. It's the dying wish of the old lion to create a way for the best and brightest to connect to solve the world's problems with three simple rules: 1.No Cost. 2.Free Speech. 3.Complete Transparency.

The animals change the world forever with their social network, THE FEED. But what happens when the animals take over the zoo? An homage to George Orwell's 1945 political satire ANIMAL FARM, THE FEED brings social media into the animal kingdom.

Infectious

The year is 2051. A Virus has run rampant on the streets claiming what hasn't been taken by rising tides. Down in the Crescent City, it's business as usual. A Garden District madam keeping a powerful secret gets mixed up in a game of cat and mouse with high-end clientele. It's only a matter of time before there'll be hell to pay.

When there is no where to run the business of being human becomes INFECTIOUS.

The Infected

After the virus threatens to destroy humanity, tribes of survivors rule the underworld. Lurking in the shadows, they hunt the healthy for resource. But after a long standing truce is broken only one member of the South Seventh gang can save her people from being wiped out. Welcome to the world of THE INFECTED.